W9-AYY-662

THE RIDDLE STREAK

Susan Beth Pfeffer

THE RIDDLE STREAK

Illustrated by
Michael Chesworth

HENRY HOLT AND COMPANY · NEW YORK

To Carl Berkowitz, Linda Emanuel,
and their two sons, Drew and Jeremy
—S. B. P.

To Punky —M. C.

Henry Holt and Company, LLC
Publishers since 1866
115 West 18th Street
New York, New York 10011

Henry Holt is a registered
trademark of Henry Holt and Company, LLC

Library of Congress Cataloging-in-Publication Data
Pfeffer, Susan Beth.
The riddle streak / Susan Beth Pfeffer;
illustrated by Michael Chesworth.
p. cm.—(A Redfeather Book)
Summary: Since her older brother always wins at Ping-Pong,
checkers, and everything else, Amy decides to learn riddles
in hope of finding some way she can beat him.
[1. Brothers and sisters—Fiction. 2. Riddles—Fiction.
3. Competition (Psychology)—Fiction.] I. Chesworth, Michael, ill.
II. Title. III. Series: Redfeather Books.
PZ7.P44855Rg 1993 [Fic]—dc20 93-14686

ISBN 0-8050-4260-1
First published in hardcover in 1993 by Henry Holt and Company
First Redfeather paperback edition, 1995
Printed in Mexico
10 9 8 7

10/05

Contents

Winning Streaks

I win!" Amy Gale's big brother Peter shouted. "That's the one hundred and seventy-second time in a row I've beaten you in Ping-Pong. And we've played one hundred and seventy-two times!"

Amy sighed. It was bad enough that Peter always won. She wished he didn't count every single victory. "I'll win someday," she said.

"No you won't," Peter said. "You won't ever beat me in Ping-Pong. I'm bigger than you are, so I'm always going to win."

Peter was bigger than Amy, all right. He was two years older and two years bigger. He always had been, and Amy was pretty sure he always would be.

"Want to play another game?" Peter asked. "I don't mind beating you again."

"I don't think so," Amy said. "I'd better go upstairs and learn my spelling words."

"I know how to spell everything you know and more," Peter said. "Ask me one of your words."

Amy tried to remember the list. "Ambulance," she said.

"That's easy," Peter said. "A-M-B-U-L-A-N-C-E. Don't you know a tougher one?"

Amy didn't even know ambulance. She thought it had two *e*'s in it. "It's not fair," she said. "You had all my spelling words already, when you were in third grade."

"I know," Peter said. "That's why I'm smarter than you too. Sure you don't want to play another game of Ping-Pong?"

"No," Amy said. "I've lost enough for one day."

"No you haven't," Peter said. "After supper, let's play checkers. I've beaten you one hundred and twelve times in a row in checkers."

"Show-off," Amy said, and left her brother in

the basement. Upstairs in the kitchen, their mother was making supper.

"Did you two have fun down there?" Mrs. Gale asked.

"Peter did," Amy said. "He beat me again."

"Someday you'll beat him," her mother said.

Amy didn't think so. She didn't think her mother thought so either. It was just the kind of thing a mother would say if her daughter had lost one hundred and seventy-two times in a row. "How do you spell ambulance?" she asked. Maybe Peter had gotten that wrong.

"A-M-B-U-L-A-N-C-E," Mrs. Gale said.

Amy shook her head. Score another one for Peter. "Mom, will I ever be bigger than Peter?" she asked.

"Maybe," her mother said. She was cutting to-matoes for their salad. "Sometimes girls get to be bigger than boys."

"If I'm bigger, will I be stronger?" Amy asked.

"If you work at it," her mother said. "You could lift weights and get to be strong that way."

"But Peter could do that too," Amy said. "Then even if I was bigger, he could still beat me in Ping-Pong."

"I don't think you have to be really strong to play Ping-Pong," her mother said. She looked up from the tomato. "What's the matter, honey?" she asked. "Does it bother you that Peter beat you in Ping-Pong?"

"He always beats me," Amy said. "I've lost one hundred and seventy-two times in a row."

"Peter!" their mother called. "Would you come up please."

Amy didn't know what her mother was going to do about Peter being bigger, stronger, and smarter. But if her mother had a plan, Amy was willing to try it.

"What, Mom?" Peter asked as he walked into the kitchen.

"Have you beaten Amy one hundred and seventy-two times in Ping-Pong?" Mrs. Gale asked.

"I sure have," Peter said. "Great, isn't it?"

"Let her win once in a while," Mrs. Gale said. "You're not going for the world record."

"You want me to cheat?" Peter asked.

"It isn't cheating if you let your little sister win once in a while," their mother said.

"Yes it is," Peter said. "It's throwing the match, and that's cheating."

Mrs. Gale sighed.

"No!" Amy said. "I don't want to win that way. I want to win honestly."

"Right," Peter said. "Just the way you lose."

"Mommy!" Amy cried.

"Then find something you both have a chance at winning," Mrs. Gale said. "So Amy can win honestly."

"There isn't anything," Peter whispered. Amy heard him, but their mother didn't. The problem was, Amy was sure Peter was right. She'd never beat him at anything. Not as long as he was bigger and stronger and older than she was.

2

???

Riddles

¶ learned this really good riddle," Amy's friend Maria said after school the next day. They were in the playground waiting for their school bus to pick them up.

"Yeah, what?" Amy asked. She liked riddles.

"What kind of person likes cocoa?" Maria asked.

"Is that the riddle?" Amy asked.

"Of course it is," Maria said. "What kind of person likes cocoa?"

"I give up," Amy said. "What kind?"

"A coconut!" Maria said. "Get it? Cocoa nut."

"I get it," Amy said. "It's not very funny."

"I don't think riddles have to be," Maria said.

"Jokes have to be funny, but riddles don't. Riddles just have to fool you."

"Well, that one fooled me," Amy said. "A coconut." She giggled. It was kind of funny thinking of a coconut drinking a cup of cocoa.

"I know lots of riddles," Maria said. "My grandfather teaches them to me. Every time I visit, he tells me some more."

"Really?" Amy asked. "They must be really old riddles if your grandfather knows them."

"He says riddles don't get older, they get better," Maria said. "Want to hear another one?"

"Sure," Amy said.

"What nationality is Santa Claus?" Maria asked.

Amy shook her head. "I give up," she said.

"North Polish!" Maria said. "That's just about my favorite."

"North Polish," Amy said. "Maria, is your grandfather big and strong?"

"I don't know," Maria said. "He's taller than my grandmother, but she's bigger."

"Does she know riddles?" Amy asked.

Maria shook her head. "She always says she leaves the riddles up to Grandpa. I don't think she knows any, except the ones he tells. And when he asks her one, even if she knows the answer, she forgets it."

"Tell me another riddle," Amy said. "A really hard one."

"They're all pretty hard," Maria said. "You didn't guess them after all, and you're just about the smartest kid in our class."

"I need one that's smarter than fifth grade

even," Amy said. "Come on, Maria. What's the hardest one your grandfather ever told you?"

Maria made a funny face while she was thinking. Amy knew Maria only made that face if she was really working on a problem. Amy knew Maria was about to tell her the hardest riddle in the whole world. She could hardly wait to hear it.

"This is a really hard one," Maria finally said. "It's my granddad's favorite, too. Ready?"

"Ready," Amy said. She was sure she wouldn't be able to guess the answer, but that was fine with her. If she could figure it out, it wouldn't be hard enough.

"You're surrounded by lions," Maria said. "Say ten lions, and tigers too, four of them, and I don't know, six leopards, and two bears. Polar bears. How do you escape?"

"I don't know," Amy said. "Are we at the zoo, maybe?"

"No," Maria said. "You're surrounded by them."

"You could be surrounded by them at the zoo," Amy said. "They could be in cages all around you."

"If they were in cages, you wouldn't have to escape," Maria said. "Give up?"

"Okay," Amy said, even though she liked her own answer about being in the zoo. "How do I escape?"

"You wait until the merry-go-round stops and then you get off!" Maria said.

"Merry-go-rounds have swans," Amy said. "Swans and ponies. They don't have lions and polar bears."

"They do if they're at a zoo," Maria said.

"But you said I wasn't at the zoo," Amy said. "That's a dumb riddle."

"It's my grandfather's favorite," Maria said. "Are you saying my grandfather is dumb?"

"No," Amy said, although she thought his riddle was. "He's real smart if he knows all those riddles."

"You didn't know any of them," Maria said. "So he must be a lot smarter than you are."

"A lot," Amy agreed. She only hoped he was smarter than Peter as well, so finally she'd find something she could beat him at.

3

???

Coconuts

"Did anything interesting happen at school today?" Mr. Gale asked as they sat in the kitchen, finishing their suppers.

"Nothing," Peter said. "Can I have more mashed potatoes?"

"May I," his mother corrected him. "And yes, you may."

"Something interesting must have happened," Mr. Gale said. "Look at all the interesting things that happened to your mother and me today." They had already told Amy and Peter about their days.

Peter thought about it. "Nothing," he said. "Great mashed potatoes, Dad."

"Thank you," his father said. "I made them from a mix."

"Great mix then," Peter said.

"Did anything interesting happen to you, Amy?" her father asked.

Amy had been waiting for that question all evening. "I learned some great riddles," she said.

"In school?" her father asked. "That's what they teach you in school?"

"No, after school," Amy said.

"First tell us what happened during school," her father said. "Then tell us what happened after."

"Nothing happened during school," Amy said. "But I learned these really great riddles afterward. Want to hear them?"

"I want to hear about arithmetic and spelling and everything else you're supposed to be learning," her father said. "But if you insist on starting with riddles . . ."

"I do," Amy said. She'd gone over the riddles

again and again since Maria had taught them to her. "What kind of person likes cocoa?" she asked.

"Your father," her mother said. "Your father just loves cocoa."

"It's a riddle, Mom, not a survey," Peter said. "That's easy. A coconut."

"I do love cocoa," Mr. Gale said. "So I guess that means I'm a coconut. Okay. That was a pretty good riddle. Now, what did you do in arithmetic?"

"We just multiplied some more," Amy said. "Here's another riddle. What nationality is Santa Claus?"

"Nationality," her father said. "That's a big word. Did you learn that word in your reading class?"

"No, it's in the riddle," Amy said. "Give up?"

"Give us a moment," her mother said. "What nationality is Santa Claus?"

"I know," Peter said.

"Finish your mashed potatoes," Mr. Gale said. "I want to see if I can figure this out. What nationality is Santa Claus?"

"But I know," Peter said.

"This isn't a contest," his father said. "Let your parents have a shot at it."

"I was never very good at riddles," Mrs. Gale said. "I'm not a puzzle person."

"Riddles aren't puzzles," Amy said. "They're riddles."

"They're a sort of puzzle," her father said. "Well, I give up. What nationality is Santa Claus anyway?"

"North Polish," Peter said. "That one is really old."

"North Polish," Mrs. Gale said. "That's kind of cute."

Amy didn't want the riddles to be cute. She wanted them to be hard. Or even if they weren't hard, she didn't want Peter to know the answers.

"I bet I know the answer to every riddle ever asked," Peter said.

"I wish you knew the answer to every arithmetic question ever asked," his father said. "Speaking of which, are you sure nothing happened in school today?"

"I'm not finished," Amy said. "I know another riddle."

"I bet I know it," Peter said.

"Bet you don't," Amy said.

"No betting at the dinner table," their mother said.

"We're not at the dinner table," Peter said. "We're at the kitchen table."

"No betting anywhere in this house," his mother said. "Amy, why don't you tell us your other riddle."

"I'm going to," Amy said. "You're in a jungle. No, I mean you're in the zoo."

"You should be," Peter said. "In a cage with all the other monkeys."

"That does it," Mr. Gale said. "Peter, you are excused."

"Excused?" Peter said. "Why?"

"Go to your room and think about why," Mr. Gale said.

"But Peter has to stay," Amy said. "He doesn't know this riddle."

"I bet I do," Peter said. "Come on, Dad. Amy wants me here."

"You're surrounded by animals," Amy said. "Lions and bears and stuff. How do you escape?"

"You're in the jungle when this happens?" her mother asked.

"No, the zoo," Mr. Gale said.

"Neither," Amy said. "I mean it doesn't matter where you are. You have to escape from all the animals."

"I know that one," Peter said.

"I knew one like that," Mr. Gale said. "Only there was nothing about a zoo. You just got off the merry-go-round."

"That's it," Amy said. "See, Peter, you didn't know."

"I did too," Peter said. "Or I would have, if you'd told it right. There aren't any merry-go-rounds in the jungle. There aren't any in the zoo, either. Boy, you're dumb."

"Go to your room right now, Peter," Mr. Gale said. "And don't come out until you're ready to apologize to your sister."

"What did I say?" Peter whined, but Amy didn't care. So what if Peter got punished? He knew all her riddles. She was never going to beat him in anything.

4
???

Sore Winner

"How about some Ping-Pong?" Peter said to Amy the next day after school.

"No," Amy said. "You always win."

"I may not today," Peter said. "My wrist hurts."

"Then why do you want to play?" Amy asked.

"It doesn't hurt that bad," Peter said. "Besides, if you win, you'll keep playing with me, and then I'll start a new winning streak."

"But what if you win today?" Amy asked.

"Then I keep my winning streak going," Peter said. "But honestly, Amy. You're getting to be a better and better player. We don't have to play for long."

"All right," Amy said. It wasn't that she wanted

to play Ping-Pong with Peter. But since he was going to beat her anyway, she figured she might as well get it over with.

They went down to the basement and got the paddles and ball. Amy loved Ping-Pong balls, how small and white and perfect they were, how they bounced when you hit them. That's why she kept playing Ping-Pong against Peter, because she loved watching the ball bounce.

"You serve first," Peter said.

"I never serve first," Amy said. "You always serve first."

"I know," Peter said. "But my wrist hurts. Just a little, but it hurts, and I want you to serve first."

Amy was sure it was a trick, but she took the ball, and hit her first serve. Peter swung wildly at it and missed. "Wow," he said. "That was a great serve."

"It was," Amy said. She and her mother had been working on her Ping-Pong game, and she was glad to see she was getting better. She served again. This time Peter hit the ball, but it missed the table altogether. It took Amy almost a minute to find where the ball had landed.

"You're playing terribly," Amy said, as she served for the third time. She had never led two to nothing before.

"It's this wrist," Peter said, shaking his right hand. He was so busy showing Amy where it hurt, he missed her serve. "That was dumb of me," he said.

Amy nodded. She was starting to like Ping-Pong.

She kept on liking it as Peter missed her serves or hit shots back wildly. When he served, Amy had no trouble hitting shots for winners. She had never played so well, and it was exciting to see just how good she had gotten.

Amy won the game easily. "Your streak is broken!" she shouted. "I've won one game in a row."

"Amazing," Peter said. "It's this wrist, you know."

Amy suspected it was too. "Sore loser," she said anyway. "Want to play again?"

"No," Peter said. "I think I'd better recover before I play with you again. I've got to get my own streak going."

"Coward," Amy said.

"I am not," Peter said. "Why can't you be happy just beating me once?"

"Because I can beat you again and again and again," Amy said. "I know it. You do too. That's why you're too scared to play with me."

"I am not scared," Peter said. "I just don't want to."

"Scaredy-cat," Amy said. "Sore loser." It figured the one time she had a chance to beat Peter twice in a row, he'd refuse to. She might never have the chance again, at least not until they were both a hundred years old.

"You won once," Peter said. "Isn't that enough?"

"No," Amy said. "You won a hundred and seventy times in a row."

"One hundred and seventy-two," Peter said.

"Well, I want to beat you two in a row," Amy said. "Come on. I bet your wrist doesn't hurt that bad. Scaredy-cat."

"My wrist doesn't hurt at all," Peter said. "I was just trying to be nice."

"Nice?" Amy asked. "You, nice?"

"I can be nice," Peter said. "Like right now, when I let you win."

"You didn't let me win," Amy said, but she wasn't so sure. She'd never beaten Peter before, at least not for a hundred and seventy-two times. "I won fair and square because your wrist hurts. Didn't I?"

Peter shook his head. "There's this guy in my class, Mike Rudolph, and he beats me in everything," Peter said. "It drives me crazy. I got to thinking maybe that's how it felt for you, losing all the time. So I let you win."

"But I don't want to win that way," Amy said. "I want to win because I beat you honestly. It doesn't count if you let me."

"That's the only way you're ever going to win," Peter said. "I'm bigger than you are and stronger and smarter. You don't stand a chance."

"Then I'm never going to play with you again," Amy said. "No matter how hard you beg."

She only hoped he would, so she could turn him down.

5

Barbie, Not Peter

Want to play some Ping-Pong?" Peter asked Amy that Saturday afternoon. It was a rainy day, and neither one of them felt like going outdoors.

"No thank you," Amy said. She was sitting in her room, sorting her doll clothes, making sure Barbie had a nice winter wardrobe.

"I'm sorry about the other day," Peter said. "I promise I won't let you win anymore."

"Not today," Amy said.

"Come on," Peter said. "You like playing Ping-Pong."

"I don't feel like playing right now," Amy said. "I'm busy."

"How about checkers, then?" Peter said. "You can be red." Peter was always red. It was his favorite color and he picked it every time.

Amy knew Barbie had a black and white polkadot dress with a jacket, but she couldn't find the jacket. The dress didn't look nearly as pretty without it.

"I don't want to be red," Amy said. Maybe the jacket was under her bed. It was amazing the stuff that ended up under her bed.

"Be black, then," Peter said. "Either way, I'll beat you."

"No you won't," Amy said.

Peter laughed. "You think you're going to beat me?" he asked. "You've never once beaten me in checkers."

"You're not going to beat me because we aren't going to play," Amy said.

"Why not?" Peter asked. "I never cheated you at checkers. I never let you win. Why won't you play with me?"

"Can't you see I have things to do?" Amy asked.

"Important things." It felt wonderful to be turning Peter down.

"Dolls are boring," Peter said. "Checkers are fun. Come on, Amy. Just a couple of games."

"No," Amy said. "If I play, you'll beat me. And then you'll tell me just how many games you've won in a row."

"But that's good for you," Peter said. "It helps you with your counting."

"I don't need any help," Amy said. "I've been counting since kindergarten."

"Then how about if I let you win?" Peter said. "The way I did in Ping-Pong. I'll play with my eyes closed or something. That way my winning streak will have to start all over again, and it'll be ages before it's big numbers."

"I don't want to win that way," Amy said. "I want to win honestly or not at all."

"But you can't win honestly," Peter said. "I'm older than you are. I always beat you."

"You won't always be older than me," Amy

said. "I'm younger and I'm a girl and you're going to die first."

"What if I do?" Peter said. "You going to beat me in checkers once I'm dead?" He laughed. "I'll be the checkers ghost," he said. "I'll come back from the grave and beat you anyway."

"I'm not going to play with you dead or alive," Amy said. "Not now, not ever. So leave me alone." She thought she saw the polka-dot jacket buried in a pile of bathing suits. Barbie swam a lot.

"How about go fish?" Peter said. "Or old maid?"

"No," Amy said.

"But I don't know how many times in a row I've beaten you in cards," Peter said. "So I can't tell you about my winning streak."

"No," Amy said. There was the jacket. Amy folded it carefully on top of its matching dress.

"Hide-and-seek?" Peter asked. "I'll be it."

"No," Amy said.

"Okay then, you be it," Peter said. "I'll hide someplace honest, but I bet you'll find me anyway. You've always been very good at hide-and-seek."

"No," Amy said. "I'm never going to play anything with you ever again, Peter. Go away."

"You'll be sorry," Peter said. "Someday you'll want to play something with me, and I'll say no, and then you'll be sorry."

"When fish can swim," Amy said.

"You mean fly," Peter said. "Boy, you really are dumb."

Amy picked up Barbie and thought about throwing her at Peter. But none of this was Barbie's fault. Amy just turned her back on her brother and waited until he left her room. She only hoped she could honestly beat him at something before the fish started flying.

6
???

Baking and Balance

Why did you have Peter first?" Amy asked her mother that afternoon. They were in the kitchen, baking a chocolate cake together. Peter and Mr. Gale were buying groceries.

"We didn't mean to have Peter first," her mother said. "It just happened that way."

"Would you have been as happy if I was first?" Amy asked.

"Absolutely," her mother said. "We didn't care if we had a boy or a girl. Just as long as the baby was healthy."

"I wish you'd had me first," Amy said. "Then I could beat Peter at stuff."

"I don't think you'd be all that happy with a

34

kid brother," her mother said. "I have a kid brother, and he used to drive me crazy when we were growing up."

"How?" Amy asked.

Her mother broke two eggs and put them in the mixing bowl. "He was always chasing after me and teasing me," she said. "Putting spiders in my bed. That kind of thing. And my mom would make me look after him. Lots of times when I wanted to be doing something else, Mom made me take Tommy along. I wanted to have a big brother, like my friend Linda, not a little brother like Tommy."

"Did Linda like having a big brother?" Amy asked. She couldn't imagine how anyone could.

"She said he bothered her sometimes, but mostly she liked it," Mrs. Gale said. "She said a big brother was a lot better than a little brother, and I think she was right about that."

"But you love Uncle Tommy," Amy said.

"I do," her mother said. "And you love Peter, whether you'll admit it or not."

"Not," Amy said, and they laughed.

"Things balance out," Mrs. Gale said. "You may not believe that now, but they really do."

"How?" Amy asked. "How does it balance?"

"Take this cake, for instance," Mrs. Gale said. She turned on the mixer, and beat cake mix, eggs, and cooking oil into batter. "Peter doesn't like to bake. So he's at the supermarket."

"Yeah," Amy said. She always enjoyed seeing the ingredients turn into a cake.

"You like baking," her mother said. "So you're here with me and we're having fun."

"Is that balance?" Amy asked.

Her mother poured the batter into the cake pans and carried them to the oven. Amy opened the oven door for her mother and watched as she carefully put the pans on the tray, making sure none of the batter spilled over.

"Balance is since you and I are in the kitchen, we get to lick the bowl," her mother said. "You take the bowl, and I'll take the beaters. Deal?"

"Deal," Amy said. Nothing tasted better than chocolate cake batter, except maybe chocolate cake itself. She licked every last drop of the batter from the bowl. Her mother did the same thing from the beaters. They both had smiles on their faces when they finished.

"I'd still like to beat Peter at something," Amy said. "I know he's going to beat me a lot more than I'll beat him, but I hate it that he beats me at everything all the time."

"I don't blame you," her mother said. "Let me think."

So Amy did. She took the dirty bowl and beaters to the sink and ran water over them while her mother thought.

"You know, I'm not so sure Peter knew the answers to all those riddles you asked the other day," her mother finally said.

"He answered them all," Amy said.

"The first two," Mrs. Gale said. "But your father answered the last one. The one about the merry-go-round."

"But Peter said he knew the answer," Amy said. "Was he lying?"

"Not lying, exactly," Mrs. Gale said. "It's just sometimes you say you know something when you really don't. You think you do, and then if you're called on, you discover you're wrong. Hasn't that ever happened to you?"

"In school sometimes," Amy said.

"Maybe that's what would have happened to Peter if Dad hadn't answered the riddle first," Mrs. Gale said. "I bet if you look hard enough, you can find a riddle Peter doesn't know. That's what you want, isn't it? Just to beat him once at something?"

Amy nodded.

"Then go for it," her mother said. "Learn a big bunch of riddles and drive him crazy!"

7

???

Riddle Research

Amy sat next to Maria on the school bus Monday morning. "How many riddles does your grandfather know?" she asked.

"Millions," Maria said.

"I mean it," Amy said. "How many riddles?"

"I don't know," Maria said. "Lots and lots. Why?"

"Do you think he could teach me some?" Amy asked.

"Sure," Maria said. "Why do you need to know riddles?"

"To beat my big brother," Amy said.

"I wish I had a big brother," Maria said. "All I have are two little sisters. They drive me crazy."

"I'll trade you," Amy said. "One big brother for two little sisters and a grandfather who knows riddles. Do you think we could go visit him after school?"

"No," Maria said.

"Tomorrow then?" Amy asked. She didn't know how long she could wait before finding a riddle Peter didn't know.

"My grandparents went down to Florida this weekend," Maria said. "They won't be back until April."

"But that's months from now," Amy said. "I need a riddle right away."

"Try the library," Maria said. "Ms. Morris knows lots of good stuff."

Amy waited impatiently until the bus finally pulled into the school. As soon as she got off, she ran to the library. There were still a few minutes before the first bell was going to ring.

"Do you know any riddles?" she asked Ms. Morris.

"What kind of riddles?" Ms. Morris asked.

"Any kind," Amy said. "Hard ones."

"How many do you need?" Ms. Morris said.

"I don't know," Amy said. "I need a riddle my brother doesn't know."

"Oh dear," Ms. Morris said. "I remember Peter when he was at the primary school. He knew lots of riddles."

"Do you remember them all?" Amy asked. "If I know all the riddles he knows, then I could maybe find one he doesn't."

"Wait a second," Ms. Morris said. "I think there might be an easier approach."

"What?" Amy asked. She had nothing against easy.

"I just got in a brand-new riddle book last week," Ms. Morris said. "Peter might know some of the riddles in it, but there have got to be a few he doesn't know yet. Let me show you the book." She looked under her desk and pulled the book out. "Here it is," she said. "*The Riddle Encyclopedia.* That sounds pretty impressive."

It was a big book and there were riddles on every page. "Can I take it out?" Amy asked.

"I don't see why not," Ms. Morris said. "You'll be the first person to take this book out. That's always an honor."

Amy didn't feel nearly as honored as she did relieved. With an entire brand-new book devoted to riddles, she was bound to come up with one Peter had never heard of.

8

Foolproof Riddles

Amy spent every spare minute at school that day copying out riddles from *The Riddle Encyclopedia*. By the time the school bus arrived at her house, she had twenty riddles carefully written out.

It was wonderful picturing Peter not knowing the answers to any of them. She could see him stammer and stumble and finally cry as riddle after riddle went unanswered. Amy wanted a riddle streak of at least ten, but fifteen, or better still, twenty seemed really perfect to her. She'd earned her streak honestly, by going to the library and doing work. It had nothing to do with being older or bigger. Those kinds of streaks didn't mean anything.

She went crazy waiting for Peter to arrive home from school. Her mother was already there, but she was working in her home office, so Amy didn't feel she could interrupt. Besides, she'd certainly find out about it at suppertime, when Peter would still be crying.

Amy waited in the kitchen, writing out a couple more riddles. There was nothing wrong with a twenty-two riddle streak, or a twenty-five one. She wondered if Peter would ever stop sobbing. She kind of hoped not.

"I'm home!" Peter shouted when he finally got in.

"Mom's working," Amy said. "Don't shout."

"I'm home," Peter whispered instead, and then he laughed. Amy laughed too. It was probably the last time Peter would laugh in his lifetime. "Want some milk?" he asked Amy.

"I had some already," Amy said. She watched

as Peter poured himself a glass. "Where do cars get the most flat tires?" she asked. She'd take him by surprise.

"At the fork in the road," Peter said. "Is there any cake left?"

"I don't know," Amy said. It was a good thing she had a few spare riddles to get her streak going. "There are cookies."

"Then I'll have them instead," Peter said.

"What goes out black and comes back white?" Amy asked.

"A cow in a snowstorm," Peter said. "No chocolate chip cookies, huh."

"Dad ate the last one yesterday," Amy said. "There are Fig Newtons left."

"I'd rather have chocolate chip," Peter said, but he took three Fig Newtons anyway.

"Why did the kid put his head on the piano?" Amy asked.

"Because he wanted to play by ear," Peter said. "Next?"

"What kind of doctor treats ducks?"

"A quack," Peter said.

Amy looked down at her list. Peter's riddle streak was definitely doing better than her own. It was a good thing she had a long list.

"What do brave soldiers eat?" she asked.

"Hero sandwiches," Peter said.

"What kind of cat works for the Red Cross?" Amy asked.

"A first-aid kit," Peter said. He rammed a Fig Newton into his mouth, then took a big gulp of milk.

"What pet is always found on the floor?" Amy asked.

"A carpet," Peter said. "Don't you know any hard ones?"

"I know lots of hard ones," Amy said. She searched her list frantically, looking for some hard ones. She was starting to feel really nervous. "What kind of house weighs the least?"

"A lighthouse," Peter said. He ate another of

the Fig Newtons. "Are you sure there aren't any chocolate chip cookies left?"

"Why did the robber take a bath?" Amy asked.

"So he could make a clean getaway," Peter said. "What did you do, study riddles at school today?"

"I know lots of riddles you don't know," Amy said.

"Sure," Peter said. "And you can beat me in Ping-Pong any time you want."

"What travels around the world but stays in one corner?" Amy asked.

"A stamp," Peter said. "Do I get to ask you any riddles?"

"No," Amy said.

"That's a shame," Peter said. "Because I took out this really good riddle book from my library last week. It's called *The Riddle Encyclopedia,* and it had lots of riddles I never knew before."

"You already read *The Riddle Encyclopedia?*" Amy asked.

"Sure," Peter said. "My librarian showed it to

me as soon as it came into the library. I read it on Saturday when you wouldn't play with me. Are you sure there aren't any chocolate chip cookies left?"

"I'm positive!" Amy shouted. She ran out of the kitchen and to her bedroom, leaving Peter behind with her list of foolproof riddles.

9

Amy's Streak

We're certainly quiet tonight," Mr. Gale said that evening as they finished supper. "Is there a reason why none of us is talking?"

"My mind's on work," Mrs. Gale admitted. "I'm sorry."

"I suppose your mind is on school," Mr. Gale said to Peter.

"No," Peter said. "I just don't have anything to say."

"What about you, Amy?" Mr. Gale asked. "Didn't anything interesting happen to you today?"

"No," Amy said. She certainly wasn't going to

tell her father she'd spent the whole day learning riddles Peter already knew.

"In that case, how about dessert?" Mr. Gale asked. "I don't suppose there's any cake left?"

"We finished it last night," Mrs. Gale said.

"I was afraid of that," Mr. Gale said. "You know, I've been thinking about that cake all day long."

"It was good," Mrs. Gale said. "Sometimes I think cake-mix cakes are better than the ones you bake from scratch."

"What did the baseball say to the cake mix?" Amy asked.

"What?" Mr. Gale said.

"It's a riddle," Amy said. "What did the baseball say to the cake mix?"

"Nothing," Peter said. "Baseballs can't talk."

"They can in riddles," Amy said.

"This is a good riddle," Mrs. Gale said. "What did the baseball say to the cake mix? I don't know that one."

"Neither do I," Mr. Gale said. "How about it, Peter? You're the riddle king around here."

"Baseball," Peter said. "Cake mix. I don't remember that one from *The Riddle Encyclopedia*."

"Give up?" Amy asked.

"One more second," Peter said. "I must know it from somewhere. I know every riddle ever invented."

"I bet you don't know this one," Amy said. "Oh, I'm sorry, Mom, about betting."

"Don't be," her mother said. "I bet Peter doesn't know either."

"Do you, Peter?" Mr. Gale asked.

"I must," Peter said. "There can't be a riddle Amy knows and I don't."

"Your time is up," Mrs. Gale said. "I want to know the answer. Amy, what did the baseball say to the cake mix?"

"Batter up!" Amy said.

Everyone laughed. Except Peter.

"I never heard that one before," Peter said. "Where did you learn it?"

"I made it up," Amy said. "Just now, when Mom was talking about cake mixes."

"Did you really?" her father said. "I don't think I ever heard a brand-new riddle before. Peter, have you ever made up any riddles?"

"No," Peter said. "I never thought I needed to. There are millions of riddles already."

"Well, now there are millions and one," Mrs. Gale said. "Amy, that's wonderful, making up a riddle like that."

"I just thought of another one," Amy said. "Knock knock."

"Who's there?" Peter asked.

"Batter," Amy said.

"Batter who?" Peter asked.

"I'm batter than you are!" Amy sang in triumph.

Amy's parents laughed. "She got you on that one," Amy's father said to Peter.

"That's not fair!" Peter said.

"Why not?" his mother asked.

"I don't know," he admitted. "But it isn't."

"I have another one!" Amy said.

"You're kidding," her father said. "Amy, this is quite a riddle streak."

"What did Porky Pig say to the silverware?" Amy asked.

Her mother, father, and brother all stared at her. It was possibly the best moment in Amy's life.

"Th . . . th . . . th . . . that's all, forks!" Amy shouted.

Everyone, even Peter, laughed. "I've got to write these down," her father said. "I'll show them off at work tomorrow."

"Me too," Peter said.

"What do you mean?" Amy asked.

"Remember that guy, Mike Rudolph?" Peter asked. "The one who beats me in everything? He knows every riddle in the book. That's why I memorized them, to beat him at riddles, but it didn't work. Tomorrow I'll try Amy's riddles on him. He's bound not to know them. It'll drive him crazy."

"You'd better tell him they're mine," Amy said.

"I sure will," Peter said. "When he hears some dumb, I mean, smart little third grader made them up, he'll really go nuts."

"You want me to make up some more?" Amy asked.

"I sure do," Peter said. "After dessert, let's go to my room and I'll write them all down."

"Amy Gale, Riddle Champ!" her mother said. "Three brand-new riddles and still going strong."

It was definitely the best moment in Amy Gale's life.